THE GIRL
FROM AWAY

CLAIRE MOWAT

THE GIRL
FROM AWAY

Illustrations by

Malcolm Cullen

KEY PORTER·BOOKS

For Winnie

Canadian Cataloguing in Publication Data

Mowat, Claire
  The girl from away

ISBN 1-55013-428-0

1. Newfoundland - Social life and customs - Juvenile fiction. I. Title.

PS8576.092V58 1992   jC813'.54   C92-094090-0
PZ7.M69Vi 1992

The publisher wishes to acknowledge the assistance of the Canada Council.

Key Porter Books Limited
70 The Esplanade
Toronto, Ontario
Canada M5E 1R2

Design: Scott Richardson
Typesetting: Indelible Ink
Printed and bound in Canada

92 93 94 95 6 5 4 3 2 1

CHAPTER ONE

"LADIES AND GENTLEMEN, WELCOME to Gander. Kindly remain seated until the aircraft has come to a full stop outside the terminal. For those passengers leaving us here, we hope you have enjoyed your flight."

The flight attendant repeated the message in French, and then bobbed down the aisle, scooping up travel pillows and earphones. "Here we are, Andrea," she said with a friendly smile. "Don't forget your tote bag and your nice leather jacket. And have a good holiday."

This was the first time thirteen-year-old Andrea Baxter had travelled by air on her own. The ticket agent had issued her a special ticket before she had boarded the plane in Toronto, with the names of her Aunt Pearl and Uncle Cyril at the bottom. In the departures lounge her mother had kissed her good-bye, and then had begun to cry when an attendant arrived to shepherd Andrea down the wide corridor leading to the plane.

Now, as the plane taxied toward the terminal at Gander airport in central Newfoundland, Andrea peered through the darkness and the light fall of snow. She could see a line-up of

1

people inside the terminal, looking out the windows at the arriving passengers. Were Aunt Pearl and Uncle Cyril there? she wondered.

Her head bent against the wind, Andrea clutched her canvas tote bag, bulging with Christmas presents, and struggled across the tarmac. Her short, wavy hair had blown every which way by the time she reached the glass door leading into the bright building. The first person she saw was Aunt Pearl, bulky in her purple and green parka and sturdy boots.

"There you be, girl!" her aunt cried, running forward to hug Andrea. The attendant smiled and handed Aunt Pearl the envelope with *Mr. and Mrs. Cyril Baxter* written on it.

"Aren't you the smart one, flying all that way by yourself!" Aunt Pearl exclaimed, as they waited among the crowd by the baggage carousel. "Were you scared?"

"No, not a bit," Andrea said firmly. "It was lovely. We had dinner and everything." She wasn't going to admit to Aunt Pearl that, for the first few minutes of the flight, as she gazed back over the retreating lights of Toronto, tears had welled up in her eyes, making the lights go all blurry. Christmas away from home. Worse, Christmas away from her mother.

But this was no ordinary Christmas. Two days earlier her mother had married Brad. She and Brad were schoolteachers. They had decided to marry in December when they both had holidays and could take their honeymoon in Florida. Brad loved Florida. Her mom had never cared for it. "It's crowded and those flat white beaches are boring," she had always said, before she met Brad.

"Aunt Pearl and Uncle Cyril would love to have you stay with them over the holidays," her mother explained, right after she dropped the bombshell about the Florida honeymoon — just for two, of course. "Honestly, darling. I talked to Pearl on the phone yesterday and she was delighted at the thought. Remember all the fun you used to have at her house?"

"But that was when I was just a little kid," Andrea protested.

"So? What's so different now? Your cousins have been growing up too. Jeff must be twelve, nearly thirteen now," her mom said reassuringly.

"But you and I always went there in the summer. It won't be much fun in the middle of winter."

"Oh, come on," her mom coaxed. "Who's the girl who loves storms? There'll be plenty of those in Anderson's Arm. More than here. You'll find all kinds of fun. Don't forget, the boys will be on holidays too."

It was true that Andrea loved winter storms. Even blizzards. Her mother and every other adult she knew grumbled about them because snow and ice made driving slippery and dangerous. But Andrea looked forward to wild days, even if she had to stay inside and watch the snow swirling horizontally past the windows of the seventh-floor apartment where she and her mom lived. Best of all, she liked to bundle up in her down-filled parka and tall boots and go out walking. She marvelled at the way the streets turned white and clean, and the way the falling snow muffled the noises of the city.

Andrea could remember being happy in Anderson's Arm on those summer holidays long ago, in the years after her dad had died. But her mom had always been there too. This time she would be far away, enjoying bright sunshine and white sand and palm trees. With Brad. Big, smiling, horrible Bradley Osborne, who seemed determined to take her father's place. "Well, he never will," Andrea told herself bitterly.

It seemed as if Brad had been hanging around their apartment forever. He had been there every Saturday and Sunday since last Christmas. Brad taught grade seven at a senior elementary school out in The Beaches. It wasn't the same school where her mother taught grade nine math. Her mom had met Brad during a professional development day. Too bad.

In some ways Brad was all right. He was always trying to be nice to Andrea, the way teachers act when you've done something clever like winning a prize for your science project. He took Andrea and her mom out to a lot of different places in his red sports car, even though there wasn't much room for Andrea in the tiny back seat. The visit to the Metro Zoo had been great. And last summer they had driven to Upper Canada Village, where people wore olden-days clothes and pretended to live in the past. That was fun, except when the village blacksmith mistook Brad for Andrea's father. How could he?

With her petite figure and wavy brown hair, she didn't look anything like gangly, blond Brad.

Most weekends she and her mom and Brad went out to eat in a restaurant, usually an Italian one. Italian was Andrea's favourite kind of food. Her second favourite was Chinese.

The trouble was, whenever Brad was around, her mom didn't act the same. She got mad at Andrea for practically no reason at all, like the time she made a lot of noise sucking her milkshake through a straw. Her mother listened so carefully to Brad, as if everything he said was important or funny, even when it wasn't. Once Brad went home, she magically zapped back to normal again, wondering what Andrea wanted in her school lunch or fussing about whether she had a clean T-shirt to put on. But the next time Brad appeared at the door, grinning and sometimes carrying one of those silly bunches of flowers, Andrea again began to feel as if she didn't matter very much.

Now Brad would be moving in. He was going to be there every morning for breakfast. Would her mom suddenly think Andrea was eating her cereal too loudly? Brad's toothbrush and shaving stuff would be littering their tidy bathroom. At night she might even have to see him wearing his pyjamas.

Lately Andrea's mom had been talking about the three of them moving to a bigger apartment. Or maybe even buying a house. That only made Andrea angrier. She didn't want to move. She liked their apartment on Willow Drive in Willowdale. The address was amusing and besides, it was the only home Andrea could remember. It had a neat balcony where you could sit in the summer and look down into the leafy backyards of a whole row of houses. There were two bedrooms, one for her mom and one for her. She had her room fixed up just the way she wanted it, with dark red Venetian blinds, a fuzzy rug on the floor, posters on the pink walls, and Gloria, her favourite doll from when she was younger, sitting contentedly in the big wicker chair.

Andrea had two close friends, one living on the fifth floor and one on the ninth, who both went to the same school as she did. If she and her mom and Brad moved away, she probably wouldn't see them anymore. And who knows what kind of room she would have in their next home. If only Brad had stayed put in his own apartment in East York, and just visited once in a while! She could have lived with that.

Andrea often thought of her own father. He had died in an accident on a construction site five years after the family moved from Anderson's Arm, Newfoundland, to Toronto. Andrea was only seven then, but she still remembered her dad.

Her mother used to talk about him a lot, always glad to answer the questions Andrea asked, although lately she hadn't mentioned him as often. His first name was Albert. Her mother had often told Andrea how musical he had been, just like all the Baxters. Most of them could sing and play musical instruments without ever having had any lessons. Andrea's father had been able to play dozens of tunes on his mouth organ. He'd also had a strong voice, and enjoyed singing in the church choir.

When Andrea was ten, she had asked her mother if she could keep her dad's harmonica in the drawer of the little table beside her bed. It was still there. Sometimes she got it out and blew into it, intrigued by the humming notes. Someday she wanted to learn how to really play it.

Her mother had a photograph album with pictures of their wedding in Anderson's Arm, and all the relatives. As well, there was a photograph of Andrea's father in a silver frame that hung beside the mirror on her mother's dresser. He and Brad couldn't have looked less alike. Her father had dark eyes and bushy, dark brown hair that was almost curly. His nose was, frankly, a bit too long. Andrea was glad that she had inherited her mother's nose. Brad had a crooked nose. He was very tall and too thin, and his blond hair was thin too. He wore glasses and had awfully big feet. He had to buy his shoes in a special store.

When Andrea and her mom had travelled to Anderson's Arm during those summers before Andrea's mom got so busy taking summer courses at university, they had always stayed with Uncle Cyril and Aunt Pearl. Cyril was her father's brother. In a lot of ways he had been like a father to her. Andrea would never forget clam-digging and picnics with him and her cousins on the beach, and the fun they had swimming in the nearby pond. But Andrea never went along when they took the dory out to catch mackerel. She was afraid of being out in a boat on the ocean; she couldn't explain why.

In the evenings Uncle Cyril usually played his accordion. He even made up his own songs. He told funny stories that made people laugh. Spending Christmas with the Newfoundland Baxters wouldn't be so bad if only her mom could be there too, instead of . . . in Florida. With Brad.

Andrea had always loved Aunt Pearl too — the comfortable woman who smiled down at her now, eyes merry behind the pale blue frames of her glasses. She liked to say that Andrea was the little girl she had never had. "I prayed for a daughter," Andrea once heard Aunt Pearl confide to her mother, "but the good Lord saw fit to send me two sons instead."

"Where's Uncle Cyril?" Andrea asked glancing eagerly from one face to another in the crowd. " Didn't he come to Gander too?"

"Oh, no, my dear," said Aunt Pearl, looking less jovial. "Cyril's away at sea. Didn't your ma tell you? He's got a job on an oil tanker."

"Yes, but I thought he was supposed to be home for Christmas."

"And that's the truth. He's supposed to be. But there's been wonderful bad weather this past fortnight, and the ship is late getting to port. Could be a few days yet."

A few days! How many days? Andrea hadn't counted on this. Christmas was only days away . . . If Uncle Cyril wasn't home, Christmas just wouldn't be right.

"Don't look so sad, my girl," Aunt Pearl comforted her. "I miss him too. But we're some glad he got steady work. After the fish plant closed down . . . well, times have been hard for us on the coast. When Cyril got a chance to sail on the tanker, he took it straight off. Way it is, he's gone for a month and then he's home for a month. Could be worse."

"How are we going to get out to Anderson's Arm?" Andrea asked, suddenly remembering that Aunt Pearl didn't know how to drive.

"I caught a ride in with Mr. Noseworthy. He got the contract to collect the mail from the airport. There he is over there."

Andrea observed a glum man with his cap down around his eyebrows and his coat collar turned up over his ears. When her duffle bag came toward them on the carousel, he retrieved it and hurried toward the door.

"Better git goin'," said Mr. Noseworthy without a smile. "Dirty weather."

For the next half hour the three of them drove along the Trans-Canada Highway in silence, while snow danced in front of the truck windshield. Then they turned onto the gravel road leading out to the bay. Aunt Pearl began chatting about the boys and the weather, but Mr. Noseworthy still didn't say much. Even with the truck bouncing along over the gravel, Andrea felt so tired that she fell asleep, her head on Aunt Pearl's ample shoulder. When she awoke an hour later, they were pulling up in front of the green and white clapboard house belonging to Aunt Pearl and Uncle Cyril. The snow had stopped and the wind had died.

Anderson's Arm looked entirely different to Andrea this time. Everything, including the road, the rocks, and the three dozen wooden houses nestled along the shore, was covered in snow. A pathway of moonlight led out across the black Atlantic Ocean. Light shone from a few kitchen windows where people were still awake. Here and there coloured Christmas lights dotted the scene like confetti. "It looks like a Christmas card," Andrea told herself, as she and Aunt Pearl climbed the slope up to the porch stairs. The only sound was the tinkling of ice crystals forming along the shore of the bay.

Although it was after eleven o'clock, Andrea could see her two cousins peering out at her through the kitchen window by the chimney.

"Rascals!" Aunt Pearl admonished them, as she and Andrea entered the warm, welcoming kitchen. "You should be in bed."

The boys, dressed in their striped pyjamas,

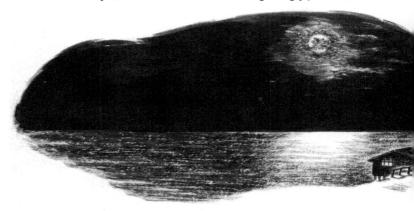

were grinning from ear to ear. Andrea hadn't seen them for three years. Of course they were more grown up now, just as she was. They both had freckles and dark hair like their dad and like Andrea's dad. Jeff, the twelve-year-old, was as tall as his mother. He had always been the shy one. Matthew, at ten, wasn't much shorter. His impish smile and mirthful eyes told the world that he was still the bolder one, the one more likely to make you laugh. Matthew was the first to speak.

"Couldn't sleep a wink, neither one of us. So we figured 'twould be best to wait up. We wanted to see Andrea as soon as she got here."

"Yes, I suppose you did, my dears. Not every day your mainland cousin comes here by her own self in an airplane," Aunt Pearl said indulgently.

"Hey, where'd you get that jacket, Andrea? That's neat," remarked Jeff, admiring her new, black leather jacket.

"Jumpin's! What a lot of zippers!" exclaimed Matthew, inspecting the zippered cuffs, zippered pockets, and the big zipper down the front. "Does everybody in Toronto wear stuff like that?"

"It's my Christmas present from my mom," replied Andrea proudly. "She bought it downtown at the Eaton Centre. She told me I could wear it before Christmas because she was going away."

"Some nice," Jeff remarked.

"Look what I see!" shouted Matthew excitedly, suddenly more interested in Andrea's tote bag full of brightly wrapped gifts than in her new jacket.

"You've got to wait till Christmas," Andrea teased, pulling the bag closer to her. "No peeking till then."

"Mom, can we have some lunch? Please, please," Jeff begged, hoping to prolong the excitement of Andrea's arrival.

"Tsk. It's late . . . Oh, all right," Aunt Pearl sighed as she filled the kettle for tea. "But only a mug-up, and we'd best be quick about it. There's half a pan of duff left from yesterday."

It didn't take Andrea and the boys long to finish the remains of the heavy pudding.

"Off you go to bed now," Aunt Pearl told them. "Up early tomorrow. There's plenty to be done."

Andrea had the small bedroom normally occupied by Matthew. Since the house was heated only by the large, black, oil-burning stove in the kitchen, there wasn't much heat upstairs. This room was much colder than her pink bedroom in the apartment back home. She hurried into bed and snuggled down under four patchwork quilts to try to get warm. Matthew had moved into the next room with his brother. The walls were thin, and she could hear them for a long time, giggling and whispering.

Chapter Two

In the morning Aunt Pearl was full of plans for the day. "Well, girl, do you want to go off with the boys and cut down a Christmas tree, or do you want to stay and make a steamed pudding with me?"

"I want to do both!" Andrea replied.

"I venture you can," laughed Aunt Pearl. "There's enough baking to last all day. You git along with the boys first and find us a proper tree."

Though the north wind was fierce, the sun shone as brightly as if it were summer, and the snow was whiter than Andrea had ever seen snow before. The three of them squinted as they trudged along the snow-covered road beside the glittering ocean.

"I know where to get a good tree, sure," Jeff announced confidently.

"Dad always got the tree other years," said Matthew wistfully, as they passed a row of fishing boats hauled ashore for the winter.

"I'm pretty mad that he's not home by now," muttered Andrea.

There was only one road through Anderson's Arm. It curved parallel to the bay and ended at the last house. From there, Andrea and her cousins had to clamber around a huge rock and follow a path that led down into a valley where there were spruce trees as far as the eye could see. How would they ever decide which one to cut?

"This one here's first-rate!" Matthew called out.

"No, b'y. That's bent crooked at the top, look," objected Jeff.

"How about this?" Andrea pointed to a taller one.

"Naah. Got all the branches gone to lee-ward," said Jeff.

The three of them finally agreed on a bushy spruce tree growing in the middle of a circle of others. Jeff chopped it down with his hatchet. He and Andrea hoisted it onto their shoulders and carried it home triumphantly. Once they

had their prize tree in the house, all fragrant and prickly, Jeff set to work building a base to hold it upright. Matthew fetched the stepladder and poked around in the attic until he found the carton of Christmas-tree decorations.

Andrea and her cousins spent the afternoon decorating the tree and helping to make the Christmas pudding.

"Tell us about your new dad," Aunt Pearl suggested, after she had set Andrea to work stirring up a scrumptious mixture of raisins, candied fruit, and maraschino cherries.

"Who, Brad? He's not my dad, but he's sort of okay, I guess."

"You call him . . . *Brad*, do you? Not *Uncle Brad* or something like that?"

"He's not my uncle, and he sure isn't my father. He's just . . . he's not like Uncle Cyril . . . Aunt Pearl, when will Uncle Cyril be coming home? Will he miss Christmas?"

"Don't fret. Ship's running late. Happens sometimes in winter. No, he won't miss Christmas altogether. There'll be fine times ahead, maid," she answered reassuringly.

Maid. That was Uncle Cyril's name for her. Andrea remembered her other visits here, when she was younger and had protested to Uncle

Cyril that she wasn't a *maid*. A maid, she had explained indignantly, was someone who came to your home and made beds or did the ironing or cleared away the dishes after dinner. "Well, maid," Uncle Cyril had replied with a wink, "if you can't do that, then I sees hard times ahead for you and your man when you git married!" After that he made up a song about her. He played it on his accordion and sang it every time she came to visit:

> *Here's a little song about this fair maid:*
> *She can't wash a dish and she can't make a bed.*
> *How will she learn what she has to do*
> *When she comes from away where the chores*
> *   are few?*

At first Andrea didn't like that song at all, but her mother took her aside and explained, "That's how Uncle Cyril and Aunt Pearl talk. When they say *maid*, they mean young girl. You should be pleased. Most people don't have a song written for them."

After a while Andrea changed her mind. She wouldn't admit it, but she was secretly glad about that song. And it had a catchy tune all right.

Christmas morning dawned with a stiff easterly breeze and a threat of snow in the slate-coloured sky. Andrea's mood matched the weather. As she crawled out from under the colourful quilts, she couldn't help but think longingly of other Christmas mornings. For six years, it had been just herself and her mom, drinking cocoa while Andrea unwrapped the many small gifts her mother had tucked into her stocking. Andrea had always hung her stocking over the back of a big chair because they didn't have a fireplace in their apartment. Toronto Christmases wouldn't be the same anymore, now that her mom had married Brad. Andrea really missed her mom. And Uncle Cyril still wasn't home.

By the time Andrea emerged from her room, Matthew had turned on the tree lights. Aunt Pearl had put out some nuts for them to nibble. Once everybody started opening presents, Andrea's downcast mood lifted for a while. Her gift from Aunt Pearl and Uncle Cyril was a beautiful hand-knit sweater in her favourite colour: a deep rose-pink. She loved every shade of pink; it flattered her fair skin and blue eyes. Jeff gave her a bottle of nail polish that almost matched the sweater. Aunt Pearl was delighted with the pearl earrings Andrea had chosen for her (true to her name, Aunt Pearl loved pearls). The boys were pleased with the gifts Andrea had brought them — a Toronto Maple Leafs hockey sweater for Matthew, and a book of pirate stories for Jeff.

With a few tears misting her glasses because

Cyril wasn't there, Aunt Pearl finally unwrapped the package he had left for her. "Oh, my. Look at this. I always wanted one," she beamed, as she held up a small, black camera, complete with a roll of film.

The last gift to be opened was the one that Brad, Andrea's new stepfather, had given her just before she left for the airport. Andrea had been grouchy about it because it took up too much space in her already full tote bag. Now she felt ashamed as she opened the package and found a portable cassette player, complete with a headset and a tape of her favourite band. How had Brad known what she wanted? She'd never dreamed she could have this and the leather jacket too.

"Let's have a listen to it!" suggested the boys, almost in unison.

"Hey, let me try it," Jeff insisted.

"What would be the good of it?" Aunt Pearl asked, inspecting the tiny machine. "Why, we've got a radio in the kitchen. When we play it, everyone can hear the music."

"But Aunt Pearl, you don't understand," said Andrea. "I can play it outdoors or in my room and listen to anything I want, and it won't bother mom or Brad or anybody."

"Well, put it aside for now," Aunt Pearl said firmly. "I want us all to watch the Queen give her Christmas message on the television."

While they watched the Queen, the wind outside died down. Pale sunlight began to filter through the clouds. On the coast, whatever weather you got didn't last long. By eleven o'clock, when the four of them were walking down the road to church, the sun was shining and Anderson's Arm looked dazzling again with its blanket of snow.

The small white church with the tall steeple was packed with people. During the Christmas service the choir sang, "I Saw Three Ships Come Sailing in on Christmas Day in the Morning." When the Baxters left the church and walked back home, however, there were still no ships to be seen on the broad horizon.

A few minutes after they reached the house, the telephone rang. It was Andrea's mother.

"Hi, Darling! Merry Christmas! We miss you. How's everything going?" exclaimed a sunny but distant voice.

"Oh, Mom . . ." Andrea sputtered, suddenly feeling as if she might burst into tears. Jeff and Matthew were sitting on the kitchen daybed, hanging on every word she said. No one had ever phoned their house from Florida before. Their wide-eyed interest in the conversation forced Andrea to regain her composure in a hurry. Her mother sounded really happy as she told Andrea about the warm, sunny weather and the beach and the wonderful food. And Brad.

Andrea didn't want to let her loneliness take the edge off her mother's joy. "Everything is fine here, Mom. We're having fun, even though Uncle Cyril is still away at sea," she reported. "And tell Brad I love my present," she said resolutely.

Later, when she and Aunt Pearl and the boys gathered to eat their Christmas dinner, Andrea knew she must try not to let them sense her despondent mood. She realized it was even harder for them, having Cyril away on this festive day. If he had been home, everybody would be laughing at his jokes and listening to his music. As it was, with everyone trying to be cheerful for everyone else's sake, the mood turned out to be a reasonably happy one. Dinner was delicious — roast turkey with savoury stuffing and loads of vegetables: cabbage, carrots, parsnips, and potatoes. Even the mashed turnips, which Andrea usually hated, tasted good that day. There was lots of cranberry sauce, made from berries that Matthew and Jeff had picked in November. And there were three different kinds of Aunt Pearl's homemade pickles. The day was almost over when they finally delved into the luscious pudding that Andrea and the boys had helped to make.

That evening Andrea was surprised to see her aunt sewing something. Surely on Christmas Day Aunt Pearl could take a holiday from chores like that.

"Little something for Matt," she explained, "to cover his face." She was sewing what looked like a piece of curtain to an old woollen toque. What on earth was it?

"We're going mummering," announced Matthew, looking pleased at the prospect.

"You've heard tell 'bout mummers, surely?" asked Aunt Pearl. "Your mother must have told you. When we were all youngsters here together . . . oh, didn't we have some times then!" She chuckled.

Andrea dimly remembered her mom talking about it. Mummering was a dress-up occasion when people went visiting from house to house at Christmas time. They were in disguise and their hosts had to guess who they were.

"Hey, Andrea, I bet you never saw a mummer," said Jeff.

"Well . . . no," Andrea admitted.

"You mean they don't have mummers up on the mainland?" Matthew asked. "Some foolish place that must be."

"We have the Santa Claus Parade, the longest one in Canada, maybe in the whole world," Andrea retorted. "And another thing, the Christmas tree down by the city hall skating rink is ten times as big as yours. I bet you never saw anything like that."

"You'll see some surprises tomorrow night all the same," Jeff promised gleefully.

"That's weird, starting the fun *after* Christmas," Andrea remarked.

"Christmas just begun, sure," Jeff insisted.

"Seems we've always had the mummers. Goes back a long ways," Aunt Pearl explained. "They last the Twelve Days of Christmas. And then they stop the sixth of January, thank goodness. Sometimes I do git tired of mopping the floor."

CHAPTER THREE

EARLY THE NEXT EVENING, WHILE Andrea was putting away the supper dishes, there was a knock on the door. Jeff hurried to answer it. Andrea heard a strange rasping voice asking, "Any mummers 'lowed in?"

Three individuals wearing a comical assortment of other people's clothes were led into the kitchen. One was tall, one was middle-sized, and one was small; all had their faces covered. The two smaller mummers had filmy cloth covering their heads and shoulders, and the tall one was wearing an old Hallowe'en mask with the face of Pierre Trudeau on it. Andrea stared in fascination at the mysterious trio.

"You can sit down, mummers," offered Aunt Pearl.

The boys observed the masked visitors carefully. Matthew started prodding one of them around the ribs, jabbing at a pillow that was tied underneath a coat several sizes too large for him. Or her. You couldn't tell.

"Mummers, do you belong up the head of the Arm?" asked Jeff.

They shook their heads, and the veils swayed back and forth.

"Down the harbour?" asked Matthew.

Another shake.

"The Cove Road? Is that where your home is?" asked Aunt Pearl.

Suddenly they heard barking outside the door. Matthew jumped up and looked out. There, illuminated by the porch light, stood Jumbo — a large black dog, wagging his tail. He belonged to the Noseworthys.

"I know who you are! I know!" cried Matthew. "Show up, you Noseworthys!"

Once their identity had been guessed, the mummers had to reveal themselves. The three of them threw back their veils. They were, indeed, the Noseworthy children. Their father was the man who had driven Andrea and Aunt Pearl from the airport. Andrea had noticed them in church — Brian, a tall, unsmiling teenager with reddish hair; his younger brother, John; and their six-year-old sister, Molly. All the Noseworthys wore jackets and boots that were too large, making them look overweight and awkward.

"Darn," muttered Brian Noseworthy. "Should've barred Jumbo in his doghouse."

"How about a song for us?" demanded Aunt Pearl. It was the old tradition that mummers had an obligation to entertain their hosts. However, once they had removed their masks, these three

suddenly became shy. At first they scarcely uttered a word. The boys looked at the floor and then
sideways at each other, trying to hide their
embarrassment. Brian finally cracked a smile, a
slightly lopsided grin that encouraged Andrea to
smile back at him. Only little Molly, who had
curly hair and a missing front tooth, gazed un-
selfconsciously around at the Baxters, a big smile
on her face.

"Has the cat got your tongue?" joked Aunt
Pearl. Brian and John still didn't say a thing.
Molly started giggling.

"Molly, my dear, is this the first time you've
been out mummering?"

Molly nodded her head vigorously.

"Well, in that case, let's see if I can find you
a little treat," said Aunt Pearl.

She cut several slices of her delicious, dark
fruitcake and passed them around. "Remember,
next time you come, I want to hear a story or a
poem," she told the Noseworthys. Finally they
replaced their face coverings and departed, first
to take Jumbo home and then to call on other
families.

More mummers came to call that evening.
Aunt Pearl and the boys managed to guess the
identities of most, but not all. One pair left as
mysteriously as they had arrived, still masked

and unknown. Andrea was intrigued. She was delighted when the boys suggested she go mummering with them the following night. They were still busy planning what they were going to wear when Aunt Pearl set out their "lunch" at nine-thirty — bread with bakeapple jam and tea.

"Mom gets this stuff at a special store in Toronto," said Andrea, spreading the amber-coloured jam on her bread. "I'm not all that crazy about it, but she is."

"Bakeapple jam? At a special store?" asked Aunt Pearl, surprised.

"Yeah. They don't sell it in the supermarket," Andrea explained, taking a sip of her tea.

"We don't get bakeapples at a store at all. We just go and pick 'em," explained Jeff.

"They're berries . . . like blueberries and foxberries and all those," added Jeff.

"Do they grow in your garden?" asked Andrea.

The boys started to laugh. They thought it was funny that anyone could imagine something wild like bakeapples growing in a garden, the same as potatoes or rhubarb. Aunt Pearl frowned at them for making fun of their cousin.

"They grow in the marsh," she told Andrea. "In every marsh. There for the taking. Last summer I put down twenty jars," she concluded. "So help yourself to some more!"

Chapter Four

"Aunt Pearl, what am I supposed to wear for mummering?" Andrea asked, as they were eating breakfast the next morning.

"No bother to find mummers' clothes," her aunt replied. "Jeff, you go to your closet. See if you can find a few things would fit Andrea. Something warm now. The wind today is colder than a merchant's heart."

"Oh, do I have to wear boys' clothes?" moaned Andrea, disappointed. "I was thinking I'd like to go dressed like . . . well, a bridesmaid or something."

"G'wan," teased Jeff. "It's only men that goes out mummering dressed like brides."

"That's mostly the way we do it," Aunt Pearl agreed. "Boys pretend to be girls. Girls pretend to be boys. Elsewise people could guess you right off. Wouldn't be so much fun then, would it?"

"Well, nobody will guess who I am," Andrea pointed out. "Nobody knows me."

"Don't be so sure," replied Aunt Pearl. "Anyone comes visiting Anderson's Arm is noticed."

That night, Andrea was so excited that she could hardly finish eating her supper. After trying on several sweaters and jackets, she had finally decided to wear a pair of Jeff's jeans turned inside out and a plaid shirt of Uncle Cyril's. The shirt was long enough to hide her leather jacket completely. She had borrowed a pair of rubber boots from Matthew. Though Andrea wouldn't have admitted it out loud, she knew she was lucky that her own boots, made of shiny black leather, were too small to fit Jeff or Matthew. She didn't relish the idea of lending her precious new boots.

The boys were both wearing long-sleeved, flannelette nightgowns belonging to their mother — a perfect disguise that adequately covered the many layers of warm clothes they wore underneath. All three mummers covered their faces with filmy squares cut from old, white, lace curtains that had once hung in Cyril and Pearl's bedroom. When they pulled their woollen caps down over their ears, the curtain material stayed in place. They could see where they were going, dimly, but no one could recognize them.

"Where d'you want to go first?" Jeff asked his brother, as the three of them made their way cautiously along the slippery road.

"How about the Noseworthys?" suggested Matthew.

Mrs. Noseworthy answered the door and hastily invited them in before the cold wind filled the kitchen.

"And mind you don't let old Jumbo in, neither," she added. The dog settled down again in his bed on the porch as the three mummers filed in and sat down. Brian and John were sitting at the kitchen table playing checkers. Molly was already in bed, and Mr. Noseworthy had gone to Gander to collect the mail. Ida Noseworthy was putting away the clean laundry. When she had finished, she sat down with her sons and they shrewdly looked over the mummers.

"Right, you mummers," she said. "I'd like a little song or dance. When I was your age, we had to entertain people before they'd give us a thing."

Jeff and Matthew got to their feet and haltingly began a clumsy step dance in the middle of the kitchen. Andrea remained perched on the corner of the daybed. She didn't know what kind of dance they were performing. She watched them with as much amusement as did Brian and John and their laughing mother who, fortunately, didn't seem to care that pools of melted snow were appearing on the kitchen linoleum.

"What's the trouble with this fellow? Can't he dance too?" asked Mrs. Noseworthy, pointing at Andrea, assuming she was a boy.

Jeff grabbed Andrea's hand, nearly pulling off her mitt, and yanked her into the middle of their crazy gyrations. All she could do was to start stomping and twisting, inventing a dance of her own, which wasn't easy when she was wearing borrowed rubber boots that were two sizes too big. But what did it matter if she did it wrong? After a few minutes of heavy-booted shuffling, they all sat down, hot and exhausted.

Right away Brian exclaimed, "I knows them, sure!"

"Who?" his younger brother asked.

"Baxters."

"Only two of 'em. Who's the other one, then?"

"Their cousin, the girl who came from away. You know, that pretty . . ." He suddenly covered his mouth with his hand, embarrassed that anyone should know he thought her pretty.

"Okay, show up, you Baxters! Show up! We knows it's you. Show up!" commanded John loudly.

Andrea and her cousins threw back the curtains that covered their faces.

"Just look at you, my dear," said Ida Noseworthy, admiring Andrea's disguise. She started taking cookies out of a round tin and placing them on a flowered plate. "I never thought to see you going around dressed like a mummer." She laughed. "But it suits you finest kind. And why not? You belong to Anderson's Arm. Born here, same as the rest us." She offered each of them a chocolate-chip cookie.

Andrea munched her cookie and said nothing. She didn't want to argue with Mrs. Noseworthy, a plump woman who seemed rather nice. But Andrea didn't think she belonged here at all. Her home was in Toronto, or at least it had seemed like home until Brad came and spoiled it.

"I knew 'twas Jeff's boots, see," said Brian Noseworthy, pointing to the boots Andrea was wearing. They looked like plain, black rubber boots identical to those worn by everyone in Anderson's Arm whenever the weather was cold and wet.

"How could you tell?" asked Andrea, puzzled.

"Easy. Patch."

"Patch?" She inspected the boots more carefully and noticed for the first time a small patch of orange-coloured rubber on the heel of one boot, covering what had been a leak.

"I minds the day Jeff put that patch onto it," Brian continued smugly. "Down in my dad's garage, in the spring of the year. He came by to get a drop of tire cement to make it stick."

"Hmmph," Jeff snorted. "I never figured you'd remember it forever and ever, amen."

"Time to git going," urged Matthew. Amid a chorus of good-byes, the three mummers trooped out into the frosty night.

"What say we call on Mr. Fudge?" suggested Matthew.

Mr. Fudge was the new United Church minister. He had recently arrived from St. John's, and everyone in Anderson's Arm knew he had yet to experience a Christmas season in which mummers invaded his home. Nobody went mummering in the city.

"No use going there," Jeff told them. "They're in St. John's visiting. I saw them drive away this morning. Hey, I've got a better idea. What say we go to the Keepings'?"

"Too darn far," protested Matthew.

Levi Keeping was Jeff's best friend at school, one of a big family where mummers were always welcome. The Keepings, however, lived at the other end of the community, a twenty-minute walk in good weather and even longer on ice-covered roads and paths.

"We can take the shortcut across the bog and then down along the shore and up over the hill. Be there in jig time," Jeff insisted.

"You tired, Matt?" Andrea asked solicitously. "Want to go home?"

"No way," said Matthew firmly.

Off they marched across the frozen bog, with reflected moonlight on the snow to show the way. The bog was nearly impassable in summer — several acres of wet land that felt as if you were walking on a field of soggy mattresses. Apart from the children who ventured there to pick bakeapples in August, most people avoided the bog until December. Then winter transformed it into a thoroughfare. The three Baxters

threw back their veils to better see their way.

"I hope you guys know where we're going," Andrea said a bit apprehensively.

"Ha. I could find my way with my eyes shut," bragged Jeff.

"I been crossing this marsh all my life," added Matthew, as they trudged over the crisp snow.

"They really are sure of themselves," thought Andrea a bit enviously. "They belong."

"Are you going to stay here all your life?" she asked the boys. "In Anderson's Arm?"

Jeff though for a moment. "I suppose. There's no better place than here."

"What do you want to be when you grow up?" asked Andrea.

"I dunno," replied Jeff.

"Ummm," said Matthew thoughtfully. "I'd like to go to sea on a big ship, like my dad."

"I know what I want to be," announced Andrea. She waited for them to ask her what, but neither did. There was only the crunching sound of their boots on the snow. Finally she stated, "I want to be an airline flight attendant. In the city, you can go to school and learn to be almost anything you want — like my mom. After Dad died, she went to university and . . ."

"Hey, what's that sound?" asked Jeff, interrupting her.

"What sound?" asked Andrea, stopping in her tracks.

"Shut up a sec. Listen!" he ordered.

The three of them stood still and listened. Then they all heard it, a long, melancholy sigh.

"Oh, my gosh," whispered Andrea fearfully. "Is that a bear?"

"Naah. Bears don't sound like that," said Jeff, trying to sound authoritative.

"When did you ever hear a bear anyways?" asked Matthew.

"Where's it to?"

"Has to be someplace handy to the beach."

"What if it's a wildcat or something and it runs after us?" asked Andrea nervously.

"Never heard of wildcats around here," said Jeff. "Okay, let's creep . . . really quiet . . . up to those rocks there. Nobody make a sound. Follow me."

At the far end of the bog was a mound of enormous rocks. Beyond that stretched Rocky Point Beach, where people went for walks in summertime and watched great waves roll in from some distant storm. Here the water was always too cold for swimming. Children, however, enjoyed themselves running along the shore and challenging one another to keep their feet dry as the breakers reached for their shoes.

Jeff climbed to the summit of the rocks first, and gazed out over the great sweep of sand, pebbles and surf. "Holy jumpin's!"

"What do you see?" gasped Matthew, trying to catch up with his bigger brother. Andrea was right behind him, clambering onto the rocks. The three of them stared into the distance. For a few seconds, they were so astonished that no one uttered a word.

"It's a whale!" exclaimed Jeff at last.

At the far end of the beach, they could see the dark shape of a whale. Its gleaming body was partly in and partly out of the water. The gigantic mammal lay motionless in the surf as waves washed over it. Then suddenly it let out an explosive, whooshing sigh that could be heard the full length of the beach.

"My gosh, it's alive!" shrieked Andrea.

"And lookit! Out in the bay," Matthew yelled excitedly. "There's another one out there. And another. And another! There's a whole crowd of them." A pod of whales was swimming around in the dark water, breaking the surface from time to time.

"What are they trying to do?" asked Andrea, clutching at Jeff's sleeve. "Are they all going to swim ashore?"

"Jaysus, they'll be stuck for sure if they don't start swimming out to sea. When a whale gets stranded like that and the tide goes out, he can't move, and he can hardly breathe, and . . ."

"Hey, come on. I wants to see him up close," Matthew called, as he climbed down over the other side of the rockpile to reach the beach.

The three of them dashed along the moon-lit shore, pounding through the wet sand in their heavy boots. The boys had to hoist the long nightgowns up around their waists so they could run. All three of the former mummers had stuffed their hats and veils into their pockets. Being mummers was now the last thing on their minds.

They were breathless by the time they got close enough to see the whale lying helplessly in the surf. Its bulky, rounded head was facing the beach, not the water.

"I sees his eye! His eye! He's lookin' right at me!" shouted Matthew, jumping up and down in excitement.

"Wow!" was all Andrea could say as she gaped in wonder at the hulking body only a stone's throw from where they stood. "It's awesome! The kids at school are never gonna believe this."

"Let's go up closer," hollered Matthew, as he danced on the shore. He was so thrilled by the spectacle that, as a big wave thundered in and filled one of his rubber boots with cold seawater, he barely noticed.

"Get back, Matt!" Andrea screamed. "If that whale rolled over, he could crush you like you were made of eggshells."

"He won't do that," shouted Matthew over the roar of the surf. "Whales don't harm people. They've got something like radar. They can . . ."

"Don't talk foolishness," Jeff yelled back. "That whale's in big trouble and won't be think-ing straight. He knows he's about to die. So don't anybody get too close."

"But we can't let him die!" Andrea insisted. "Jeff, we've got to help him get free. What can we do?"

The boys just stared at the motionless whale. Finally Jeff spoke up. "There's nothing we can do. Look at the size of the creature. 'Twould take a tow truck to shift him an inch."

"But if we go for help as quick as we can . . . there might be something somebody could do," Andrea pleaded.

"No harm trying," said Jeff, though he sounded doubtful. The three of them ran to the other end of Rocky Point Beach, where they had to cross a field of beach grass and climb a small hill before reaching the main road.

"What kind of whale do you suppose he is?" Andrea panted, as they paused to catch their breath. "He's black all over, has a kind of round head, and he's long, nearly as long as . . . a streetcar. No, not that long. As long as a stretch limousine, I think."

"How long is a stretch limousine?" asked Jeff, mystified.

"How long is a streetcar?" asked Matthew.

"Oh, honestly!" cried Andrea, forgetting that her cousins had only seen those things on television and weren't sure of their size.

"We got a book at home, and it has pictures of all different kinds of whales. I can find out what it is," said Jeff confidently.

Just then they saw headlights approaching along the road a short distance away. "Hurry. Let's see if we can hitch a ride," called Matthew, starting to run again.

"My mom said I was never to hitch-hike," Andrea protested.

"Aw, come on. You want to help the whale or not?" Jeff cried in exasperation. "And anyway, Matt and I are here to protect you."

They recognized Mr. Noseworthy's truck, on its way back from Gander with the mail.

"Mr. Noseworthy! Mr. Noseworthy!" they yelled from the roadside, frantically waving their arms.

He slowed and then stopped and peered at them suspiciously out the side window. The boys were still clothed in long nightgowns. Even though Mr. Noseworthy had known them all their lives, he did not immediately recognize them. As soon as he did, however, he opened the truck door on the far side.

"Get in, then," he invited glumly. "Tired of going around mummers, eh? Too far to walk home?"

"No, no, you don't understand." They were all shouting at once as they climbed up and crowded into the front seat beside Mr. Noseworthy.

"A whale!"

"Stranded on the beach!"

"Long and black!"

"Can't move!"

"Seems like he can't breathe."

"He could die!"

"We gotta get help!"

"Beached whale, you say?" Mr. Noseworthy summarized, when he could get a word in. "Now that's a fine kettle of fish. Just what are you figurin' to do with him?"

"Don't know for sure. Maybe push him back out to sea," Jeff said earnestly, still a little breathless. Then he thought about how big a job that would be. "Well, not us. We got to get more people to help."

"It's possible that when the tide is high, a few hours from now, that whale might be able to swim away," Mr. Noseworthy mused as he changed gears. He steered the truck around the corner and rumbled up the Cove Road hill toward the Baxters' house. "A whale used to fetch a good price one time. You didn't think about that now, did you? Be worth more dead than alive. That's a lot of meat."

"Meat? You mean to eat?" asked Andrea, horrified.

"No, not fer us," he replied. "But, one time around here you could sell the meat to the mink farm for feed."

"What mink farm?" asked Jeff.

"You never heard tell of the mink farm? Gone now, of course. Before you was born. There used to be a fellow had a mink ranch down at Rattling River. Fur was a good price them days. I heard he made a nice bit of money."

"Ewww, that's disgusting," exclaimed Andrea, but her voice was lost amid the commotion as the truck stopped outside the Baxter house. Everyone scrambled out and hurried inside.

"Mom! You won't believe what we found . . ."

Quickly the boys related their amazing discovery.

"We're wondering what kind of whale it is," finished Andrea.

"A shame Cyril's not home just now. He'd know for sure," lamented Aunt Pearl.

"Oh, I really, really *wish* Uncle Cyril was here," said Andrea with a sigh.

"Pothead whale, I reckon," remarked Mr. Noseworthy. "'Twas the same thing a few years back down in Trinity Bay. They come ashore now and again. Nobody seems to know why."

"Where's that book Dad has, the one with all the different whales in it?" asked Matthew.

"Right here, slowpoke. I found it," said Jeff, who was already leafing through the pages, looking at the illustrations of all the world's whales.

"Let's see . . . we've got beluga whales, blue whales, fin whales, killer whales, minke whales

. . . I don't see any pothead whales," Jeff said, as his brother leaned over the book with him to inspect the pictures.

"Got some other name in the book. Pilot whale. That's what they call it," snapped Mr. Noseworthy.

"Pilot whale. Sure, look. Here it is," announced Jeff triumphantly, holding up the book so they could all see the picture. "That's just like the one down on the beach. Flat nose and everything."

"Read us what it says," requested Aunt Pearl.

"'*Pilot whales. The origin of the name is not clear, but it may derive from the whales' habit of following schools of herring, thereby piloting fishing boats to good fishing grounds. Pilot whales are one of the smaller species, and are found in all seas of the world. They frequently beach themselves, often* en masse. *Marine biologists are still not certain why this happens.*'"

"What's 'en masse'?" asked Matthew.

"It's French. It means a whole bunch all together," replied Andrea smugly.

"So what they mean is the other whales we saw might come ashore too," Jeff concluded.

"What can we do, Aunt Pearl? That whale is going to die unless we can somehow shove him out," said Andrea. "And what about the others?"

"There's nothing to be done tonight," said Aunt Pearl. "It's dark and it's late. We can't go round waking everyone. Besides, I wonder if anyone can help anyway."

"Maybe we should call the Mountie," suggested Mr. Noseworthy.

"Mountie couldn't do much, could he now? In the first place, he'd have to drive out here from the detachment at Seal Brook. Likely be midnight before he got here. And then what?" demanded Aunt Pearl.

"He's got a gun. I say 'twould be best to put that creature out of his misery," said Mr. Noseworthy gravely.

Aunt Pearl sighed and considered the matter for a moment, as Andrea and her cousins stood in anxious silence. "Well, someone could do away with the poor thing, I suppose. But then we'd have a dead whale on the shore. Stop and think about that, Isaac Noseworthy. The remains could still be there years from now. And the smell would knock you over before it finally rotted away."

"Got to be some use for him," Mr. Noseworthy insisted.

"Nothing I heard about," responded Aunt Pearl. "That mink ranch went out of business fifteen years ago. Even when it was a going concern, they never had a big enough freezer to hold all a whale's meat. Would only be wasteful if that poor beast died, and a proper nuisance."

"And horrible," added Andrea.

"The youngsters got the right idea. Best thing we can do is get that whale out of there alive," said Aunt Pearl.

"But how?" asked Jeff.

"Blessed if I know," replied Aunt Pearl. "But first thing in the morning we can all get to work on it."

CHAPTER FIVE

NOT EVEN THE LEADEN EASTERN SKY could dampen the excitement in the house next morning. The whole family was up and diving into breakfast by six-thirty. That was much earlier than the boys ate on school mornings. This day, however, nothing could have kept them in their beds.

The phone rang at quarter to seven. It was Isaac Noseworthy reporting that he had already driven down to the beach. The whale was still there and Mr. Noseworthy had been close enough to observe that the animal was still breathing. In the pre-dawn light, Mr. Noseworthy thought he had seen signs of other whales out in the deeper water.

"You know what? I bet the whales out in the bay are trying to talk to the one on the beach," announced Andrea.

"Talk?" laughed Jeff. "A whale can't talk."

"Oh, you know what I mean. Whales have underwater sounds they make, that other whales understand. I saw it on TV one time. I figure they must be worried about the one stranded on the beach. I think they care," Andrea said wistfully.

The boys stared at her, uncertain whether they shared her sentiment or not.

"I think I will give the Mountie a call before we head for the beach," said Aunt Pearl, opening the telephone directory. "He'll be awake by now. Like as not we'll need to round up some people to help. And listen to me, all of you," commanded Aunt Pearl. "Everyone dress warmly. There's snow in that sky. Andrea, you borrow one of the boys' hats."

"I hate wearing hats," Andrea said.

"You'll be glad of a hat. You could be out there all day and no place to get warm," Aunt Pearl warned.

Grudgingly Andrea accepted a toque that had the words *Montreal Canadiens* knitted into it. She shoved it into her pocket.

"And you'd better borrow Jeff's old rubber boots again. And extra socks," Aunt Pearl added, glancing at Andrea's stylish leather boots. "If seawater gets into those, 'twould be the end of them in a hurry."

"Oh, all right," grumbled Andrea as she pulled on the patched boots. "Aunt Pearl, why don't you bring your new camera? You could get a picture of the whale."

"To tell the truth, I'm not altogether sure how to make it work," admitted Aunt Pearl.

"I can show you. Mom has one just like it," Andrea reassured her.

"I'll bring it then," Aunt Pearl agreed, and then turned to pick up the phone.

Aunt Pearl and Mrs. Ida Noseworthy rode in the cab of Mr. Noseworthy's truck, while the Noseworthy and Baxter kids sat in the open back. They arrived at Rocky Point Beach just as snow began to fall. Andrea soon saw that they were far from alone with the unfortunate whale. News had travelled through Anderson's Arm faster than a northeast gale. The Keeping family was there, including all eight children. Even the three trouble-making Abbott boys had joined the crowd, looking less menacing than usual at this early hour. Men, women, and children were hurrying down to the cold beach to marvel at the sight of a whale with its body in the ocean and its massive head resting on the shore. Snow flurries obscured the seascape, making it impossible to see if other whales were still swimming in the deeper water of the bay.

"There's all kinds of them out there," Matthew assured everyone who spoke to him. "Last night, in the moonlight, it was clear as noon. I was the first to spot them."

"You were not. I saw the whale first," Jeff insisted, shoving his brother into the sand.

"Yeah, but I saw the offshore ones first," Matthew sulked, brushing sand from his jacket sleeve.

At 8:30 a tall Royal Canadian Mounted Police constable arrived. He looked cold, trudging doggedly across the beach from his car. The earflaps of his cap were down, and his dark blue nylon jacket was dotted with snowflakes.

"Sorry I'm late, folks. Took darn near an hour to drive here from Seal Brook. The visibility was practically zilch some places because of the snow squalls."

"Morning, Constable Wheeler," said Mr. Noseworthy, stepping forward to greet the Mountie. "We're just trying to figure what's best to do with this poor creature. I figured it would be best to shoot him and put him out of his misery, but . . ."

"Looks like a heckuva problem," agreed Constable Wheeler, peering at the unlucky whale through the snow. "To tell you the truth, this is the first time I ever saw a whale. I only got posted here last summer. I'm from Flin Flon, Manitoba. If it was a moose in trouble, I'd have a better idea what to do."

"We don't see that many whales ourselves, not on the beach like this," explained Mr. Keeping, a lobster fisherman. "Oftentimes we see them when we're out in boats, but they try to stay clear of us."

"I put in a call to a marine biology professor, a Dr. Elliott at Memorial University, before I left the detachment," reported the Mountie. "She's an expert at saving whales that get into difficulties. She told me she'd come herself as soon as possible."

"Take a nice while to get here, driving all the way from St. John's," observed Mr. Noseworthy.

"Well, she said she'd try to get a ride in a government helicopter. But by the look of that sky, I don't figure they'll be doing much flying," Constable Wheeler concluded.

"Might be too late," observed Jeff gloomily.

"The important thing, according to Dr. Elliott, is to keep the whale wet," said the Mountie. "If the skin gets too dry, that can cause dehydration. So, until we can figure some way to get him back in the ocean, we've got to organize a bucket brigade." He raised his voice. "I'd like you all to go home and round up every bucket you can. Put on waterproof clothes, if you have some, and rubber boots. Then get back here as fast as you can, okay?"

The Baxters, Noseworthys, Keepings, and others who had gathered on the beach hurried to put the Mountie's plan into action. Meanwhile new people kept arriving, eager to see the stranded whale. They stepped closer and closer, daring to touch the smooth, black skin, to marvel at the great head, to admire the broad tail, so much like the tail of an aircraft in its shape.

The high tide during the night had kept the whale partly afloat, but now the tide was receding, increasing the animal's peril. Without the buoyancy provided by the ocean water, the weight of the whale's great body began to press heavily on its lungs. Its breathing became laboured, and soon it was gasping for air like a person suffering from an asthma attack. Its breath, reported those close enough to catch a whiff of it, smelled like a hundred dead fish.

Immobilized, the frightened whale could only blink its tiny eyes as it gazed — seeing or perhaps unseeing — at the curious people watching it. From time to time it thrust its flippers back and forth across the damp sand. The effort was useless, however, and did nothing to budge its heavy body from its sandy prison.

"Does he know we mean to help?"

"A whale is a knowing creature."

"Looks poorly to me."

"His days are numbered, I'd say."

"Has to be a way to launch 'im off."

"They say he's got buddies out in the bay."

The challenge of trying to return the lonely whale to the sea soon united the community. Mr. Keeping and several others were wearing hip waders and rubberized jackets when they returned to the beach, ready for action.

"Won't do a pick of good if he dies here, will it now?" declared Mr. Keeping, addressing the crowd. "Best for everyone — ourselves and the whale too — to get 'im out of here alive."

It didn't take long to form the bucket brigade. Every able-bodied soul in Anderson's Arm wanted to help. The volunteers formed a long line across the beach from the surf to the stranded whale. Then they began passing along buckets of seawater from one pair of hands to the next. It was a wet job, and exhausting. Andrea soon realized she had never worked so hard in her life. Her arms ached. Despite the cold and snow, she was sweating, not freezing. She grabbed bucket after heavy, sloshing bucket from solemn Brian Noseworthy, who stood to her left. She swung each bucket over to Jeff, on her right. He, in turn, passed it to Matthew — and on and on, until it finally reached Mr. Keeping.

Moses Keeping had been chosen to stand beside the whale. He was the tallest man there, and had strong arms from years of hauling lobster traps into his boat. He took on the job of

splashing bucket after bucket of cold water over the whale's back.

"Hey, watch it, clumsy!" scolded Andrea, as Jeff accidentally spilled some water inside her boots. They were the same old boots she had borrowed to go mummering, and were too big for her. Quite a lot of water splashed in.

"Ooops. Sorry. But it's only water," Jeff retorted. "I can think of worse things."

"Now my feet are all cold and clammy," Andrea complained. Swiftly she bent over to scoop up a handful of wet snow. She shoved it inside the collar of her cousin's jacket.

"Stop that!" yelled Jeff, flailing his arms at her.

"Quit carrying on, you two," ordered Brian Noseworthy, passing Andrea another full bucket. "We got a job to do here."

Constable Wheeler insisted that each person in the bucket brigade take a break every thirty minutes. Near noon, he took a breather himself and hiked back to the road where he had parked his car. Turning on his police radio, he called the police dispatcher to try to find out when Dr. Elliott might arrive. By then the falling snow had turned into swirling squalls that, every few minutes, obscured everything on land and sea.

Finally the Mountie received a message from Gander that the helicopter and Dr. Elliott were grounded there. Snow and high winds were making it dangerous to travel even by road. The police wanted to know what weather conditions were like at Anderson's Arm.

"Weather's no better here," replied Constable Wheeler, "but if we don't get this whale out on the high tide tonight, I'd say it's game over."

There was static on the police radio. "I'll put the doctor on. Hold on," came a distant voice. Soon a new voice could be heard. "Constable? This is Alison Elliott speaking. Here's what I suggest. Get hold of a boat, a sturdy one with a strong engine. And you'll need lots of rope. You've got to get a line around the whale's tail. Once the tide comes in and the whale is partly submerged, there's a fair chance that the boat can pull away until the whale is afloat. Do you understand?"

"Might be possible, ma'am," replied Constable Wheeler doubtfully.

"And you mentioned this morning that there were other whales near by. Is that correct?" asked Dr. Elliott.

"Yes, the kids who discovered the whale last night claim they saw more of them swimming out in the deep water. But there's so much snow this morning, we can't see if they're still there," said the Mountie.

"Most likely they are. Pilot whales live in extended families. If one gets stranded, the rest will stay nearby, and often end up on the shore too. It might be the leader who's on the beach," explained Dr. Elliott.

"Leader?" asked the Mountie. "How can you tell if he's the leader? One whale looks much like another to me."

"That's our problem. Whales do look the same to us. But the whales know who their leader is," said the faraway voice of the scientist.

"So that makes it even more important to get our beached visitor launched," said Constable Wheeler. "We sure don't need any more of them. Thanks. Over and out."

The Mountie plodded back across the wide beach. "We're going to need a boat, a sturdy one with a strong engine," he explained, as the whale watchers gathered around and the bucket brigade took a break. "Any of you folks got one?"

"Well, me son, I'd say most of us here got a boat of one kind or another," replied Mr. Keeping. "But fishing season's been over since November, and our boats all been hauled ashore. 'Tis a day's work to get one back into the water and fit to go to sea."

"There's one boat still in the water," offered Mr. Noseworthy reluctantly. "It's me old trap boat. Used to fish with her one time, but now Brian and I just take her down to the brook where we cut our firewood."

"Noseworthys' is just about the last house that's got a wood stove," Jeff explained to Andrea. "Rest of us all got oil nowadays."

"Isaac Noseworthy's kind of set in his ideas," whispered Aunt Pearl. "He likes the old ways."

"Thanks, Mr. Noseworthy," said the Mountie. "That's generous of you. Now, if you can show me where you keep your boat . . ."

Mr. Noseworthy and his son Brian headed for the truck. Aunt Pearl sent Andrea with them to borrow a dry pair of boots and socks at the Noseworthys' house. "Like as not you'll catch your death of cold, girl," she scolded, when she discovered how wet Andrea's feet were from all the water that had splashed in. "Wouldn't want you sick when we send you back to your mother and your new stepfather."

"Foolishness," muttered Mr. Noseworthy, as he turned the key to start the truck's engine.

"What's foolish?" asked Brian, who was sitting beside him.

"Still wonder if 'twouldn't have been the best thing all round to shoot that poor creature," grumbled Mr. Noseworthy, as the truck went slowly along the snow-covered road.

"No!" Andrea protested. "We have to try to save him. We absolutely have to. Suppose that whale was somebody we knew. One of us. Wouldn't we lie there hoping and praying to be rescued?"

"Hmmph. That might be. But he's sure sufferin' a long time for the sake of some wonderful idea that scientist up in St. John's has got."

Constable Wheeler followed the Noseworthy truck in his police car. Mr. Noseworthy parked the truck beside his house, and then got out and headed down the path toward the cove where he moored his boat. Andrea and Brian and the Mountie followed him. They, in turn, were followed by Jumbo, who had emerged from his doghouse wagging his tail, pleased to see some of his family returning home.

The *Rosebud* was nearly the same length as the whale. The vessel was old and scruffy and needed a coat of paint. There was a small cabin in the bow of the boat, but the rest was open. The bottom boards were littered with bits of bark and twigs from the load of logs that had been her most recent cargo. The boat was tied to a small, rickety wharf that Mr. Noseworthy called his "stage."

The wet snow was turning to spits of rain as Constable Wheeler scanned the *Rosebud*. He observed that there was no water in the hull, which told him there were no leaks. She looked seaworthy. So did the ancient engine, which her skipper was coaxing into action by turning a heavy wheel. At first it shuddered and coughed, but soon settled into a steady, reassuring CHUG . . . CHUG . . . CHUG . . . CHUG . . . CHUG . . . CHUG . . . CHUG . . . CHUG . . . .

"Got some strong rope, Skipper?" called the Mountie.

"Finest kind. Right in me store there," shouted Mr. Noseworthy, gesturing toward a weathered grey shed beside the stage.

The Mountie stepped inside, gathered up several coils of rope, and hurled them into *Rosebud*'s forward hold.

"All aboard what's coming aboard!" bellowed Mr. Noseworthy over the thudding of the engine.

Brian climbed aboard quickly and Jumbo followed in after him.

"I thought you was planning to come too, Mr. Mountie," hollered Mr. Noseworthy, who suddenly seemed younger and more vigorous now that he was at the helm of his vessel.

"No thanks, Skipper. I got my work cut out for me on the shore."

"What about you then, girl?" Mr. Noseworthy called out to Andrea, who was standing uncertainly on the stage.

"I don't think I . . ." Andrea began.

"Come on. You been actin' like a fish out of water ever since you landed in Gander. You're the one with all the sympathy for that whale. Get on board with us. See what you can do to help."

Andrea stared at him, astounded. She hadn't thought of Mr. Noseworthy as a particularly perceptive person, but he was right. She did feel like a fish out of water in Anderson's Arm. She hadn't realized it had been so obvious to others, even to Mr. Noseworthy, of all people.

Constable Wheeler was becoming impatient. "What's it to be, Andrea? You can catch a ride back to the beach with me. Your aunt will be expecting you."

Andrea had always been leery of boats, especially grubby-looking ones like the *Rosebud*. She stood for a moment longer, wondering what to do. Then she turned to the Mountie. "No, thank you. I don't need a ride. I . . . I'll go in the boat with them. I want to help that poor whale find his way home," she said resolutely. Then she added, "All I really need is a dry pair of boots."

"I'll get you some, and socks too," responded

Brian, leaping back onto the stage and running up toward the house.

"And fetch an oiled jacket for her as well," called Mr. Noseworthy. "No sayin' what the weather's going to do."

In a matter of minutes they were off. Mr. Noseworthy manoeuvred his boat out of the narrow cove and into the bay. Soon he was steering through choppy seas toward the point of land marking the beginning of Rocky Point Beach. Anderson's Arm looked quite different from the water.

For the first few minutes, Andrea was a little afraid, but she was relieved to find that the *Rosebud*, though unimpressive looking, moved solidly through the water. Being out on the water wasn't nearly as scary as she had expected. She was glad that she had taken Aunt Pearl's advice about dressing warmly and wearing a hat. She

was grateful that Brian, who was turning out to be rather thoughtful, had found her a pair of dry rubber boots as well as a pair of thick, hand-knit socks. He had also found a fisherman's yellow jacket for her. Though it smelled oily and was too big, it did protect her new leather jacket and kept it dry.

As soon as they rounded the point, the boat headed into the wind and the waves, and every few seconds a shower of spray soaked them. When Andrea licked her lips, she could taste the salt.

Shivering, she huddled next to big, furry Jumbo, who was perfectly at home travelling in a boat, sitting quietly on the wooden seat between Andrea and Brian. His fur was wet with the snow and salt spray, which made him smell like an old mattress that had been left out in the rain. It didn't seem to matter though. He was a great source of shelter and warmth.

"Look! There's a whale," shouted Brian suddenly.

Without warning a huge head had broken the surface of the water, not far from the boat. Then an explosive blast of air and water vapour shot upward. A fin rolled by, and then the sleek, black mammal glided silently back into the depths.

"Thunderin' Jaysus!" exclaimed Mr. Noseworthy, adjusting the engine to its slowest speed.

"They're still out here!" cried Andrea.

"How many whales was it you and your cousins saw yesterday?" asked Mr. Noseworthy.

"I don't know exactly," she replied. "But I think it must be the beached whale's family. They must be terribly worried about the one who lost his way."

"That might be, but we don't want to run into any of 'em," said Mr. Noseworthy, pondering the situation. "Brian, you keep a watch out to starboard. And you, maid," he directed Andrea, "keep an eye out to port."

Maid. There was that word again. Andrea shrugged. This was Newfoundland, and they used expressions that most people had never heard in Toronto. But she understood, now, what Mr. Noseworthy and her relatives meant. Newfoundlanders sometimes had another way of saying things. She felt rather pleased that they were treating her as one of their own. She huddled down in her position on the left side of the boat, concentrating on watching for more whales.

"We don't have to worry, Mr. Noseworthy," said Andrea. "My cousins told me that whales have radar. They know where we are, and they won't run into us."

"Seein' as our old boat got no radar, we won't be taking any chances," Mr. Noseworthy replied.

The three of them stared silently into the dark, rolling ocean. Even Jumbo was alert, his nose twitching as if at the scent of an unfamiliar animal. In a few minutes another whale made its graceful ascent from the cold depths. It sprayed a fountain of steamy vapour over them, and then noiselessly disappeared as they watched in fascination.

Luckily the snow was diminishing, so Andrea and the Noseworthys could now partially see the shoreline, the helpless whale, and all the people standing around. The boat made its way closer and closer to the beach, bobbing and rolling in the lively motion of the surf. Mr. Noseworthy flung his anchor over the side. "Close enough," he exclaimed. "I don't want the *Rosebud* beached like that whale there."

"Attention, Skipper, can you hear me?" came a metallic-sounding voice from the beach. It was the Mountie talking through a loudspeaker.

The crew of the *Rosebud* didn't have anything like a loudspeaker to use to call back. All they could do was shout in unison and wave their arms. "Yes! Yes! We hear you!" they cried. Even Jumbo barked.

"Right," replied the faraway voice of Constable Wheeler. "Next thing is to get one end of your rope to the shore. See if it will float."

Brian started uncoiling the heavy rope that lay in the forward hold.

"Hang on there, Brian, me son," Mr. Noseworthy called. "Way the wind is, 'twould likely carry it out to sea. I don't rightly know how we're going to get that rope ashore. The water's too deep for anyone to wade out from the beach and take it."

"Could somebody swim out for it?" suggested Andrea.

"Swim?" asked Brian incredulously. "A person would freeze to death in two minutes."

"All I meant was . . . if somebody had a scuba-diving suit, or something," explained Andrea, trying not to sound like an idiot.

"Or a fur coat like Jumbo," said Brian thoughtfully, patting the dog.

"Well sure, why not Jumbo? He could go," Andrea suggested.

The three of them stared at the dog, who wagged his tail, pleased at the sudden attention.

"My mom told me that when she grew up here, back in the old days, they had this dog, a big dog," explained Andrea. "And he would swim out in the ocean and retrieve things. I saw a photo of him. He looked something like Jumbo, but with a white chest and feet."

"Jumbo can swim with the best of them," agreed Mr. Noseworthy, fondling the dog's ear. "Yiss, Jumbo, old boy. I thinks we got a job for you."

News of the stranded whale had been broadcast over the radio, and the crowd ashore was now growing larger. A dozen people from nearby Round Harbour had arrived in the back of the truck that was used for snow ploughing. Several more had come on their snowmobiles from the small community at Rattling River. A television crew from St. John's was attempting to reach Anderson's Arm. Their journey, however, had been stopped at Gander.

"Probably just as well the road is closed," Constable Wheeler told himself. One thing he didn't need to contend with was a huge throng of sightseers. He had more important problems on his mind. Just how were they going to tie up the whale and tow it into the water?

"Who would like some tea?" asked Aunt Pearl, bustling along with a big thermos and some plastic cups. Mrs. Noseworthy was right behind her with a large bag full of molasses cookies. There had been no time for a meal at noon, so Aunt Pearl and Ida Noseworthy had gone home to fetch cookies and make tea.

Constable Wheeler helped himself to a large cookie, munched it, took a second one, and then aimed his loudspeaker at the *Rosebud*. "Attention, Skipper. We're ready to receive the line!"

Mr. Noseworthy had finished fastening a light rope to his dog's collar. "Jumbo, old man, here's your chance to be a hero," he announced. He strained to lift the heavy dog, hoisted him over the side of the boat, and lowered him into the icy water.

CHAPTER SIX

THERE WAS A SPLASH, AND THEN A sodden Jumbo looked up at his master, indignant and surprised. He paddled around in a circle close to the boat, barking noisy demands to be hauled back aboard. Jumbo loved to swim, but nobody had ever dumped him so rudely over the side of a boat into a wintry sea.

"Go, Jumbo, go!" screamed Andrea, worried that the dog might freeze to death. But Jumbo only barked and whined and scratched at the side of the boat, his brown eyes pleading.

"No, boy, no! Go to shore!" Brian gestured, pointing to the beach.

But Jumbo wanted to be on board the *Rosebud* with his family. He looked forlorn and frustrated, as if he thought that suddenly nobody loved him.

On the beach, the villagers were straining their eyes as they watched the drama of the bewildered dog. One of the boys from Rattling River had a pair of binoculars, and a woman from Round Harbour had brought a small telescope. Jeff and Matthew and other bystanders took turns looking through these devices so they could see better.

"Constable Wheeler, why don't you call the dog through your loudspeaker?" suggested Aunt Pearl.

"What's his name?"

"Jumbo."

"JUM-BO! HERE, JUM-BO!" bellowed the Mountie through his loudspeaker. One after another, the other people joined in. "HERE, JUMBO! HERE, JUMBO!" they began chanting like a chorus.

Jumbo was growing cold and tired from swimming in circles. When he heard his name being called, he figured somebody wanted him, even if his family on the *Rosebud* didn't. The big dog turned and began to swim toward the voices on the shore. As the distance between dog and boat increased, the coil of rope started to unfurl. Jumbo paddled determinedly on, swept forward at intervals by the surging waves. The skipper

and his crew watched in silence, too tense to utter a word. No one wanted to say what each was thinking: what if Jumbo didn't make it?

"Here comes the dog," called the Mountie urgently, as Jumbo approached. "Who'll volunteer to wade out for the rope?"

"Right. Let's go," said Moses Keeping to his neighbour, Alf Rose. Both men were wearing hip waders and rubberized jackets. They waded out into the cold seawater, waving their arms at the weary dog. "Over here, boy," they called.

Jumbo had no need of encouragement. By then he could see the beach ahead of him, and he was swimming furiously to reach it. Mr. Keeping had to grab him by the collar to stop him.

Quickly the two men wriggled the collar over the dog's head. Then they let him swim untethered toward the shore. Soon Jumbo was in shallow water, where he could wade. On the shore dozens of excited people crowded around the bedraggled dog. Unceremoniously Jumbo shook himself, splattering cold water all over his admirers.

"This dog deserves a medal!" exclaimed one woman.

"He must be perished with the cold," said Matthew, taking off his woollen scarf and trying to dry Jumbo's fur with it.

"Some smart!" exclaimed Aunt Pearl, patting Jumbo's soggy head as she gave him a molasses cookie.

"Moses! Alf! Can you get that line around the whale's tail?" shouted Constable Wheeler, standing at the water's edge.

"Yessir, we'll give it a try," they yelled back. Alf Rose quickly untied the rope from the collar the two men had taken from Jumbo's neck. They reeled the light rope in until the heavy tow rope Mr. Noseworthy had fastened to its other end finally reached them. Then they sloshed through the breakers over to the whale's tail.

"You get on the far side of 'im, Alf," called Mr. Keeping. "We got to pass the line around his flukes."

"And what if he decides he don't like the idea?" enquired Mr. Rose. "Wild creatures don't like to be tied, you know."

"Not much he can do, is there now? Can't run away; he's got no legs. Can't bite us; he's got no teeth," replied Mr. Keeping.

Stooping on either side of whale's tail, the two men passed the loop of rope around the narrowest part, between the flukes and the body. Then, with frigid water slapping at the shoulders of his rubberized jacket, Mr. Keeping made it fast.

Suddenly the whale swung his broad tail up and then swiftly down with a great splash. The men leapt back, startled. At the same time the frightened mammal let out a mournful sigh.

"Me son, I told you he wouldn't like this," said Mr. Rose nervously.

"More likely in a hurry to get out of here," remarked Mr. Keeping as he double-checked his knot. Then he hollered to the constable, who was observing them from the beach. "She's fast!"

"START PULLING!" shouted Constable Wheeler to the crew of the *Rosebud* through his loudspeaker.

On board the boat, Mr. Noseworthy hauled up the anchor and then shoved the engine into gear. "Full ahead!" he roared. Andrea didn't know what to expect next. But she hung on tightly as the *Rosebud* headed for the open sea. White water from the labouring propellor churned under the stern. The tow rope lifted out of the water as the vessel tugged at the bulk of the partly submerged whale.

A series of towering waves tumbled in, and the whale began thrashing its tail. It rolled slightly to one side as another big breaker crashed on the beach. Then suddenly it was afloat, but barely. Before the weary, terrified whale had time to think of its next move, it was being towed — tail first — into deeper water.

"The whale is swimming! 'Tis off to sea! It's saved!" shouted the excited people on the beach, who had been eagerly watching the drama unfold.

"Not quite free yet," said Constable Wheeler, training his binoculars on the *Rosebud*, which was slowly proceeding out to sea. "They still have to get that line off the whale."

The *Rosebud*'s engine strained against the immense weight of the whale. It was attempting to swim now, arching its back and spouting weakly.

"He's in some rush to join his buddies out in the bay," Mr. Noseworthy speculated.

"Maybe it's a girl whale," said Andrea. "Everybody's been calling it *he* but it could have been *she* all along."

"Your guess is as good as mine," the skipper responded. "Only another whale would know for sure." He turned to his son. "Brian, you bide back here and take the tiller. It's time to get that line off."

It was late afternoon by this time. The snow had stopped falling, but the sky was growing dark and the *Rosebud*'s crew could barely see the beach behind them. Brian sat at the stern, holding the boat on course with the engine going slowly, while his dad began hauling in the rope that was tied to the whale. The *Rosebud* and the whale drew closer and closer together, until they were almost parallel.

Mr. Noseworthy leaned over the side of the boat, peering down into the dark green water as the whale came alongside. It was barely moving now, exhausted after its long ordeal.

"You'll be leaving us, old fella, soon as you're clear of the rope. Just as well we didn't shoot you," said Mr. Noseworthy softly. He stood up and fastened a length of nylon rope to a cleat on the afterdeck. Then he tied the other end around his waist.

"Now listen here," he told Brian and Andrea. "In case I fall overboard, you youngsters haul me in again."

"Oh, Mr. Noseworthy. This is dangerous. I'm scared!" cried Andrea.

"Don't be fearful. Be careful," he replied. Then he grasped the gunwale with one hand and leaned out over the side. Thrusting his arm down into the ice-cold water, he groped for the end of the rope that held the whale captive. Suddenly a wave surged over his head and shoulders. Dripping with water and gasping for air, he heaved himself back onto the deck for an instant. After catching his breath, he tried again, this time leaning out even more precariously, reaching deeper into the water. Coughing and sputtering, Mr. Noseworthy hauled himself back a second time. This time he was clutching the end of the tow rope.

"Head for home, Brian," he commanded, half-choking with salt water.

"You did it, Dad!" exclaimed Brian with one of his rare grins.

"She's free! Our whale is free!" shouted Andrea.

The three of them watched the black body glide smoothly underneath the boat toward the open ocean and freedom.

"I've done a lot of jobs in me time," said Mr. Noseworthy, busily wringing the water out of his jacket, "but fishing around underwater after some whale's tail sure takes the cake." He looked around the boat at the shivering youngsters, and then gave Brian a course to steer for Rocky Point, barely visible in the fading daylight.

CHAPTER SEVEN

 EARLY THE NEXT MORNING, THE TELE-vision crew finally arrived. There was no whale for them to photograph, however. All the whales had disappeared. The camera people scanned the horizon with binoculars, but there wasn't a trace of a spout or fin or tail.

Fortunately, Aunt Pearl had a whole roll of pictures of the beached whale in her camera. The producer was delighted to use them.

"Just imagine that!" she told Andrea joyfully. "My first camera and my first roll of film, and my pictures are going to be on television."

That evening the host of the six o'clock television news told the story in a dramatic voice. "The citizens of Anderson's Arm had to act on their own yesterday to save the life of a beached pilot whale." A film clip of Andrea, Jeff and Matthew appeared on the screen, and the announcer continued, "These young people were the first to sight the stranded whale."

"Jumpin's, it's us!" shouted Matthew in the Baxters' parlour, where the family was watching.

"Shut up and listen!" snapped Jeff, poking him in the ribs.

"Because a blizzard forced the closure of the

Trans-Canada Highway," the announcer explained, "the concerned people of this small community received little outside help in their attempt to save the life of the whale. Constable Fred Wheeler of the Seal Brook detachment managed to reach Anderson's Arm, but bad weather grounded a helicopter carrying marine biologist Dr. Alison Elliott."

Even though Aunt Pearl's photos had been taken through falling snow and were a bit fuzzy, the black whale could still be seen lying in the sand. The dark shapes of people surrounded it.

"Using a local boat and the effort of many volunteers," said the announcer, "the people of Anderson's Arm were finally able to haul the whale out to deeper water, where it appears to have rejoined its companions. During the night this lucky whale and its pod evidently fled from the shallow bay and swam safely out to sea."

There was a panoramic shot of the now-empty Rocky Point Beach with not a whale or person to be seen on it. This was followed by a shot of Mr. Noseworthy patting Jumbo as the two of them posed beside the *Rosebud*.

"So all's well that ends well for whales in Anderson's Arm," the announcer concluded with a cheery smile. "And now over to you, Debbie, and the sports."

"Thanks, Ted. Last night in Atlanta . . ."

Aunt Pearl snapped the television off and announced that supper was on the table and growing cold. "No time to waste. The mummers are still on the go. I want to have us fed and the kitchen tidied just in case anyone drops by."

"Mom, can we go out mummering again?" asked Matthew, stifling a yawn.

"Mummering indeed. Haven't you had enough excitement? Some other night, perhaps, but certainly not tonight. Now then, Andrea, you dig in."

"Oh, boy. Jigs dinner!" cried Jeff enthusiastically.

"Well, seeing as this has been a special day, I figured you boys . . . and Andrea . . . deserved a treat." Aunt Pearl smiled.

What Andrea was really longing for was a pizza with everything on it, even though she knew there was no pizza takeout place in Anderson's Arm. As soon as she got to Toronto, she told herself, that was the first thing she was going to eat. Only a few more days, and she would be home with her mom again. And Brad. She stared at the plate set before her. It was loaded with boiled vegetables — turnips, cabbage, and potatoes — and little bits of some kind of meat dotted here and there. It wasn't remotely what she wanted, but she was starving. It didn't take her long to finish her plateful.

"What kind of dinner did he call it?" Andrea asked Aunt Pearl, putting down her fork.

"Why, Jigs dinner, of course. Boiled dinner. You mean to say your mom doesn't cook this for you up in Toronto?"

"No."

"Well, she ate lots of it herself when she was a girl. Every Sunday, sure."

Jeff and Matthew had also finished theirs, and were already back at the stove for a second helping when suddenly there was a loud BANG BANG BANG on the storm door.

"Goodness," clucked Aunt Pearl. "Who's coming to call when we haven't even cleared the table yet? Matthew, you go and see who it is."

Matthew opened the door to face a solitary mummer — a large figure wearing a heavy jacket and work pants, with a towel tied clumsily over his head.

"Come in, Mummer," called Aunt Pearl. "We haven't finished our supper, but you can bide for a minute." She inspected him carefully. "Sit down, and we'll try and guess where you belong."

"Is it somewhere along the Arm?" asked Jeff.

The mummer made a gruff snorting noise, but didn't answer the question.

The boys stared at the towel-covered face. Jeff exchanged a glance with his mother. Then Matthew got a sudden fit of the giggles, but stifled it when Jeff jabbed him in the ribs with his elbow.

"Well, Mummer. Seems you don't have much to say for yourself," observed Aunt Pearl. "How's about you sing or dance for us?"

"Yeah. Yeah!" yelled the boys.

"I got an idea. Jeff, you go upstairs and fetch your father's accordion," Aunt Pearl suggested.

Jeff bounded up the stairs, returning in a flash with the shiny instrument. Andrea was surprised. Imagine lending Uncle Cyril's accordion to this stranger! He might not know how to play it. He could even break it.

The mummer hoisted the accordion strap over his shoulders and started fingering the keys, still with his gloves on.

"What song you want?" he whispered hoarsely.

"Oh, just whatever comes to mind," Aunt Pearl said with a smile.

He started to play. He played as if he had been doing it all his life. What was he playing? Andrea thought the melody sounded familiar. Suddenly it dawned on her. It was "Here's a Little Song About This Fair Maid." But how did the mummer know that tune?

All at once it struck her. "It's Uncle Cyril!" she shrieked.

"It's me all right. Got here as quick as I could!" he cried, yanking the towel from his head.

"Dad! Dad!" the boys squealed, leaping toward him. "We knew it was you! We knew right away."

"Our little joke," Aunt Pearl explained, patting Andrea's arm. "Cyril called earlier to say he'd be home this evening. So we decided, what

with it being the time for mummers and all, to surprise you and the boys."

"Oh, Uncle Cyril!" Andrea gasped, not sure whether she was laughing or crying. "I'm so glad you finally got here. You missed Christmas and I was so . . ."

"Christmas hardly begun, sure!" Uncle Cyril exclaimed, snatching her up and whirling her around the kitchen as if they were at a dance. "Just you wait, maid, fine times still to come."

That night Andrea snuggled down under all her quilts as a rising wind rattled the panes of glass in the window. She felt so happy. At last Uncle Cyril had come home. She had helped save a whale's life. She had overcome her fear of boats. And the fun of Christmas in this surprising, wonderful place wasn't over even yet.

Such a short while ago she had been reluctant to come here. Now she was in no hurry to leave. In a funny way, maybe she did belong here.

CHAPTER EIGHT

"ANDREA! ANDREA! HERE WE ARE!"

Her mom was waving from the midst of a crowd of people in the arrivals lounge of Toronto's Pearson airport.

"Mom!" sobbed Andrea, running to hug her mother. For a moment she couldn't say another word because she thought she might really start to cry.

"And here's Brad," said her mother, beaming up at her new husband.

"Hi there, kiddo," smiled Brad. "How was your trip?"

"Oh, it was great! I've got so much to tell you," said Andrea.

"We have a lot to tell you too," replied her mother happily, as they headed for the parking garage and Brad's red car. The newlyweds both had suntans, and were wearing matching, bright-yellow shirts under their winter coats. Their flight had arrived earlier that afternoon from Daytona Beach.

"Oh, Sweetie," said her mom, throwing her arm around Andrea's shoulders. "You know, I was so worried about you after your flight took off for Newfoundland. Being there in the winter isn't the same as summer, with picnics and everything. I got thinking maybe you'd find it boring."

"Mom, I wasn't bored. I was . . ."

"Brad and I decided," her mother interrupted, "that next Christmas we'll all three go to Florida. You'll love it. Can you imagine going swimming on Christmas Day? It was something else."

"Mom, I've got an even better idea," countered Andrea.

"What's that?"

"Next Christmas, let's all go to Anderson's Arm."

"Ah, come on," laughed Brad. "You mean to say we'd have more fun in Anderson's Arm than in Daytona Beach? What a kid!" He chuckled as he reached forward to grab her duffle bag so he could carry it out to the car.

"You know something, Brad? You just might," Andrea replied solemnly.

"That's my girl," smiled her mom. "I guess you've found your roots are in The Rock."

Tears sprang to Andrea's eyes. It was true. During those last few days in Anderson's Arm, she had really begun to feel at home, the way she imagined the whale felt back in the ocean. Not that there weren't things she missed about Toronto. Like takeout pizza.

By the time they reached the car, Andrea had decided. She would try to meet Brad halfway, no matter how difficult it was. She knew her attitude toward him diminished her mother's happiness. She had been too selfish.

"You know one reason for us all to visit Newfoundland?" she asked, sliding into the back seat.

"What's that, Sweetie?" asked her mother.

Andrea swallowed hard. "Well, Uncle Cyril and Aunt Pearl haven't met my new stepdad yet. Maybe they should."